A Mouse in Winter

A Mouse in Winter

UPPITY'S STORY

ANNE MERRICK

Pictures by Tessa Richardson-Jones

FOR SAM AND HARRIET

First published in Great Britain in 1996

Bloomsbury Publishing PLC, 2 Soho Square, London W1V 6HB
A CIP catalogue record for this book is available from The British Library
ISBN 0 7475 2661 3 pb
ISBN 0 7475 2662 1 hb

10 9 8 7 6 5 4 3 2 1

Cover design by Alison Withey
Typeset by Hewer Text Composition Services, Edinburgh
Printed and bound by Caledonian International Book
Manufacturing, Glasgow

Key to mouse Parlours
1 Uppity
2 Calamity
3 Homity and Dimity
4 Alacrity
5 Serenity
6 Curiosity
7 Serendipity
8 Dignity
9 Oddity
→→→→ Tracks
Wild Wood
4
Harry's room
5
Kitchen
7
Cellar
9
Underground Spring

Manor House
The Village
2
3
Attic
Jones's Bedroom
Parlour
6
8
Foundations

CHAPTER ONE

In the Outhouse next to the kitchen, Mr Jones was searching for something.

He tugged at a heavy wheelbarrow in the corner and staggered back as a pile of rusty tools jangled across the floor.

'Drat!' said Mr Jones. 'Dang this load of old junk!'

And leaving it in a heap he stepped into the Yard. Frost nipped at his fingers and nibbled his toes. Over the rooftop the sky was the colour of iron.

Blowing on his hands he crossed the Yard and poked his head through the open kitchen window.

'Mrs J,' he said, 'Isn't it time for elevenses? The smell of those pies is driving me crazy. And how about a drop of rum in my coffee to warm me up!'

'Hot grog for the Cap'n!' croaked the Parrot, swaying around her cage like a drunken sailor. 'Hot grog for the Cap'n!'

'Hot Dog?' barked the Dog, leaping up from his basket. 'Did somebody say HOT DOG?'

'Mr J,' said Mrs Jones, setting a tray of hot mince pies down on the table. 'See what you've started!

All this racket will make my blessed cake sink. Now close the window, do – while I take a peep at it!'

So Mr Jones shut the window and stood with his nose pressed to the glass while Mrs Jones opened the oven door.

'Hurray-and-HUP-she-rises!' cackled the Parrot.

And indeed the cake was rising perfectly, its top bubbling like a cauldron and already beginning to brown.

Wiping her floury hands on her apron, Mrs Jones smiled at Mr Jones. But inside her head she was seeing her small grandson whose eyes were as blue as the summer sky and whose hair shone black as a raven's wing.

'Won't be long before Harry's here,' she said to Mr Jones as she opened the window and gave him a pie. 'I reckon it's going to be the BEST Christmas ever.'

CHAPTER TWO

Behind the stove in the kitchen, there was a cavity in the wall and in this cavity lived Great-Great-Grandfather Serendipity.

Because he was the oldest and largest and wisest of the Mice who lived in the house, Serendipity had the most comfortable Parlour in the whole Mousehold. Dried moss, the colour of fox's fur, carpeted the floor and in the warmest corner there was a couch made from a scrap of red velvet that once, long ago, his wife Charity had nibbled out of the Jones's curtains.

When the sweet, fruity fragrance of Mrs Jones's cooking drifted into his Parlour, Serendipity was dozing on his couch. His nose twitched, his mouth watered and he sat up, wide awake.

'Mince pies,' he murmured. 'Already!'

And his old bones ached at the thought of winter.

Hobbling across his Parlour he peered out in to the dusky passageway that wound through the wall from the kitchen to the Attic. A crowd of up-and-coming young Mice were scurrying down the track. They were tumbling over each other and tripping one another up as they hurried to be first.

'My dear Children,' said Great-Great-Grandfather, stepping out on to the path and barring the way with outstretched paws, 'I hope you are not going to forage in the kitchen! Not in a CROWD like this! Not in BROAD DAYLIGHT!'

The Mice shuffled to a halt and hung their heads.

'But Grandad,' said Uppity who was the boldest of them, 'it's quite safe. Mr and Mrs Jones are as blind as bats and as deaf as a doorpost! *They* won't know we're there!'

Serendipity shook his grey head.

'How many times,' he said, 'do I have to remind you that this house is OUR WORLD. And if we want to survive in this world we must avoid all DANGEROUS SITUATION situations . . .'

There was a stir in the crowd and Uppity's cousin Curiosity pushed her way to the front.

'What's happening?' she asked. 'Why has everyone stopped?'

Nobody answered her because Great-Great-Grandfather was going on and on about how lucky they were to live in the Jones's house where there were plenty of tit-bits but no TRAPS and no CATS.

'Oh boring, boring,' muttered Uppity, who as well as being bold was sometimes rather rude. He was trying to think of a way to sneak past Serendipity and escape to the kitchen, when he felt a tug on his tail.

'I want a story, I do,' piped a small voice. 'Ask Grandad to tell us a story . . .'

Uppity groaned. He had forgotten he was supposed to be looking after his sister. He scowled at her but she dodged past him and hopped straight up to Great-Great-Grandfather. A beam of light from his Parlour lit up her sandy coat and Serendipity, who was especially fond of her, patted her head gently.

'If you want a story, little Hopalong Cassity,' he said, 'you shall have one.'

When she was very young one of Cassity's legs had been crushed in an accident. She was playing Tag with her cousins in the Attic when a great clap of thunder shook the house to its Foundations. A heavy encyclopedia slid from the top of a rickety pile of books and crashed on to her paw. Ever since then she had been lame. But she never complained or let it stop her from doing anything . . .

'What sort of story shall it be?' Serendipity asked her. 'A fairy tale – or a scary tale?'

'A scary one,' said Cassity, with a shiver of delight.

'Yes, yes,' cried the others, pressing forward eagerly. 'Tell us a *scary* one, Grandad.'

Then, before Uppity could argue or escape, he found himself ushered with the others into Great-Great-Grandfather's Parlour. Settling them around him in a circle, Serendipity twiddled his whiskers while he thought for a moment.

'Many, many moons ago,' he began at last, 'long before any of you were born, this house was HAUNTED.'

'Ooh,' breathed the little ones. And they cuddled up close to one another.

'It was haunted,' continued Serendipity, 'by a black-hearted Mouse whose sole delight was to tease and torment. And because of this he was called MALIGNITY . . .'

Uppity, who was sitting between Cassity and Curiosity, jiggled up and down. He did not much like stories – unless they were about fighting. And as for Ghosts – he did not believe in them!

'Whenever the moon and stars were set,' said Serendipity, 'Malignity stole out of his lair in the Cellar and crept up to the kitchen. He scrabbled behind the skirting board and squeaked

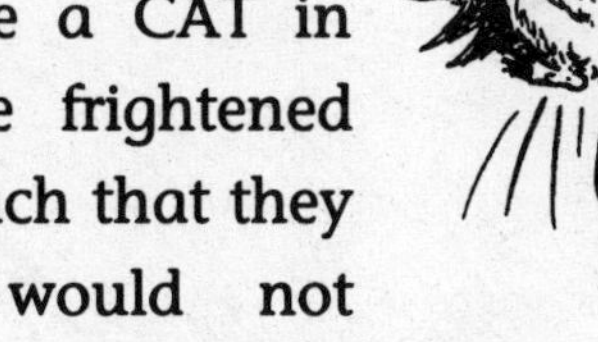

behind the door. He hoo-hooed like an OWL in the chimney and miaowed like a CAT in the cupboard. He frightened all the Mice so much that they would not go into the kitchen to forage. And everywhere he went he breathed out an icy cold that froze them to the bone . . .'

As Serendipity's story droned on and Mrs Jones's cake filled his Parlour

with its tantalising brandy-wine smell, Uppity grew more and more restless. He started to have an itch. First it tickled his nose, then it tickled his tummy and then it tickled behind his ear.

Raising his leg to scratch himself, he saw that his sister was sitting absolutely still. Her paws were clasped beneath her chin and she was completely lost in her listening.

Carefully he wriggled himself out from between her and Curiosity and keeping his head low he backed on to the track. He paused for another scratch and to make sure he had not been missed. Then he scampered away towards the kitchen.

CHAPTER THREE

The kitchen was deserted. Mr Jones was in the Outhouse, Mrs Jones was upstairs, the Dog was in the garden and the Parrot was fast asleep in her cage.

'Huh!' said Uppity. 'I *knew* it would be safe enough!'

And he dashed across the floor to forage under the table. He found a blob of sticky cake mixture, half a sugared cherry and a curl of apple peel. He was so busy nibbling that it was some time before he realised that someone close by was singing.

'What is Mrs J made of? What is Mrs J made of?' sang the someone. 'Sugar and spice and all things nice. That's what Mrs J's made of!'

Gulping down the last sliver of apple, Uppity turned round and saw his Uncle Serenity boogeying underneath Mr Jones's rocking chair. He was snapping his paws and wiggling his bottom and rolling his eyes. When he noticed Uppity watching him he stopped for a moment.

'Get with it, Man!' he wheezed. 'It's Party time! Help me jazz things up a bit!'

Uncle Serenity was rather lazy and very greedy but he was the most cheerful Mouse in the whole Tribe and he was always ready for a bit of fun. So Uppity joined in and they both sang at the tops of their voices while they rocked and rolled all over the kitchen.

'That was groovy, Man!' puffed Uncle Serenity when at last they reeled to a stop.

He fanned his face with a dead geranium leaf and then beckoned Uppity to follow him into the larder. Leading the way past his own Parlour behind the bread bin, he showed Uppity the marble shelf where rows and rows of Mrs Jones's mince pies were cooling on a wire rack.

'There, Man!' he said. 'How's that for a Feast!'

It was much, much later when Uppity remembered his sister. The sherry in the mincemeat had gone to his head and long before he got back to the kitchen, he collapsed beside a sack of the Dog's Bonios, and fell asleep.

When he woke there was no sign of Uncle Serenity and his head felt as heavy as a stone. He crept into the kitchen. Mrs Jones was in there now, sweeping the floor. Keeping close to the skirting board Uppity made for the gap which led to the track in the wall. He was just about to squeeze through it when his cousin Homity poked his head out from the other side.

'Boo!' said Uppity, and Homity squealed.

'Bet you thought I was the Ghost!' scoffed Uppity.

Homity was so timid that if he saw his own shadow he ran away in fright.

'Actually,' said Homity, his whiskers quivering, 'I thought you were Cassity. She came to the kitchen to look for you ages ago – after Grandad finished his story. And she hasn't come back.'

'Snarls!' said Uppity. 'Where can she have got to?'

Leaving Homity and keeping a wary eye on Mrs Jones and her broom, he searched all round the kitchen. But he could not see Cassity anywhere and she did not answer when he called. When he came to the door to Outside he saw it was wide open, so he went out on to the step and looked into the Yard.

Uppity knew that in spite of her limp his sister could move fast. And she was so venturesome that although he would never have admitted it, he sometimes thought she was braver than he was.

'Cass!' he called. 'Are you there?'

Again there was no answer and he was just sniffing about, trying to pick up her trail, when close behind him he heard the swish-swoosh-swish of Mrs Jones's broom. Before he could move out of the way, something tickly and prickly brushed across his back and he was swept right off the step and sent rolling across the yard in a cloud of dust.

Coughing and sneezing, he scrambled to his feet.

But he was still staggering round in dizzy circles when Mrs Jones slammed the door shut – and locked him out.

CHAPTER FOUR

Outside the grey of the sky was spreading like a stain and it was already nearly dark. The flagstones in the Yard chilled Uppity's paws, and a bitter wind ruffled

his fur. For a while he scampered to and fro trying to keep warm. Then he huddled in the roots of the apple tree that grew against the kitchen wall.

Looking up he saw what he thought were white feathers spiralling slowly towards him through the bare branches of the tree. The feathers drifted down on to the flagstones where they disappeared as soon as they landed.

Uppity stared at

them until their twisting fall made his head spin. But when he looked down again he saw that they were no longer vanishing as they fell. They were beginning to gather and spread across the Yard, like a sparkling, white carpet.

'So that's it!' he said to himself. 'Snow!'

Although he had never seen snow Uppity knew all about it from Great-Great-Grandfather's stories. He knew that the carpet of snow would soon thicken and deepen, piling up around him until he drowned in its soft, white coldness. He must look for somewhere better to shelter.

He scrambled out of the tree root and scurried along in the lee of the house wall. He skirted a drain and then a wooden trough where the brown stalks of last summer's geraniums were blossoming now with flowers of snow. At last he came to the door of the Outhouse and snuffing along its splintery base he discovered a crack just wide enough to let him in.

Back in the kitchen, Mrs Jones put away her sweeping brush, took off her apron, and went to draw the curtains.

She saw the snow whirligigging in the Yard. And she heard the North Wind howling around the walls.

'You can huff and puff as much as you like,' she said to it. 'But you won't blow *this* house down!'

As she went to put the kettle on the hob, she looked at Mr Jones, asleep in his chair beside the stove.

'Bless my soul, Mr J,' she said. 'You're quite worn out! But won't Harry be excited when he sees what you found in the Outhouse!'

Mr Jones rocked gently but did not wake. He was deep in a dream of himself as a Boy. Beneath him a dapple grey horse rocked and swayed as they galloped together, racing the wind through the leafy green glades of the Wild Wood . . .

Most of the up-and-coming young Mice believed Uppity was fearless. But it was easy enough to seem brave when there were plenty of other Mice around. Here, alone in the cold and dark of the Outhouse, it was different.

Coal dust lay everywhere. It gritted the floor and grimed the walls. And it clung to the cobwebs that hung like curtains across the window panes so that hardly a gleam of light passed through them.

Trying to show himself that he was not afraid, Uppity hummed Uncle Serenity's song and swaggered a little as he started to cross the floor towards the fireplace.

According to the legends of his Tribe, there was a secret passageway that linked the Outhouse chimney to the chimney in the Smallest Bedroom, where his cousin Alacrity lived. As he reached the middle of the Outhouse, he could hear the North Wind hoo-hooing like an Owl in the chimney. How he wished that Alacrity or Cassity – or even Homity – was with him!

The darkness grew denser than ever and he quickened his pace. But then he ran headfirst into a bucket, bruising his nose.

'Snarls!' he said.

As if his speaking had disturbed someone, he heard a rustle from somewhere above his head.

'Who's that?' he squeaked.

There was another rustle and then a well-known voice said, 'It's all right, Uppy. It's me – Hopalong!'

Uppity took a deep breath.

'Cass,' he said crossly. 'Whatever are you doing

in here? And where *are* you? You sound as though you're flying about in mid-air!'

'Not flying,' giggled Cassity. '*Riding*. I'm on Trojan's back.'

'Trojan?'

Uppity stood up on his hind legs, trying to see his sister. As he did so he noticed that he was very close to something which towered above him from the centre of the floor. Dropping on to all fours he moved around it until he could see it outlined against the pale square of the window. Then he stopped and stared in astonishment.

For there, right in the middle of the Jones's Outhouse, was a HORSE.

The Horse was not standing on its own feet. It was spread-eagled on a wooden frame, its out-stretched legs prancing in a frozen gallop. Its neck was proudly arched, its head held high. And sitting between its pricked up ears was Cassity.

'Come down, Cass!' said Uppity. 'You can't stay there all night!'

There was something about the Horse which he did not like. It was so silent and still. And in the blackness its grey flanks seemed to shimmer with a strange light of their own.

He heard the uneven patter of Cassity's claws on wood and a moment later she was slithering down the frame.

'I was looking for you, I was,' she said as she landed beside him. 'And I saw Mr Jones come in to the kitchen and tell Mrs Jones he'd found his old rocking horse, Trojan, under the woodpile. I wondered whatever a rockinghorsetrojan could be so I snook out here to see. But Mr Jones came back and closed the Outhouse door and then . . .'

'Oh boring, boring!' said Uppity. 'I don't want to hear the whole story! We must get back into the house. If we stay here much longer we'll turn into Ice Mice!'

Ever since he had come into the Outhouse it had been growing colder and colder. Already he could feel his whiskers stiffening as his breath froze on them. Nudging Cassity ahead of him, he set off once more towards the hearth. But they had hardly gone a tail's length when they heard a scrabbling, squeaking noise behind them. And then a muffled groan, that seemed to come from *inside* the Horse.

'Snarls,' he said. 'What was that?'

'Poor Trojan,' murmured Cassity, turning round. 'He's so unhappy, he is! I'd better go back . . .'

Knowing how soft-hearted his sister was, how she would grieve over a Beetle whose wing was broken, or spend ages comforting a Spider whose web Mrs Jones had brushed away, Uppity grabbed one of her ears between his teeth before she could move. Then, in spite of her struggles and protests, he dragged her across the floor, over the hearth-stone and into the grate.

CHAPTER FIVE

Up and up they climbed. Damp soot clogged their paws and sometimes drifts of black ash blocked their way. The chimney twisted and turned. And it was so dark that they could not even see the shine of each other's eyes.

Just as Uppity began to think they would never find their way out, he turned a corner and his paws slid from under him. Then, with Cassity clinging to his tail, he rolled helter-skelter down a steep slope and in a tangle of tails and whiskers, they both shot out into the hearth in the Smallest Bedroom.

Alacrity, who lived with her family in a cupboard in the wall, was frolicking on the hearth rug. She heard a rumble in the chimney. Then she saw a Monster with eight black legs and four red eyes tumble into the empty grate.

'Hickory, dickory,' she cried, backing away. 'It's Malignity!'

'Don't be such a bug-brain, Ali!' said Uppity, sorting himself out from his sister and spitting out cinders. 'It's only us!'

He ran up and down, trying to shake the soot from his coat.

'Wait till your Mam sees you,' laughed Alacrity, frisking around them. 'You look more like Moles than Mice! She'll be as mad as a Bee in a bottle!'

Uppity and Cassity lived with their mother, Gravity, in the old Doll's House in the Attic. Most of the up-and-coming young Mice lived among the lumber in the Attic. And although it was a long way from the kitchen where they went to forage, it was a good place to live. The sun and the moon shone into it through the skylight and through gaps under the eaves they could see right across the Jones's garden and over the Water Meadows to the Wild Wood on the rim of the World.

The Doll's House had a rather plain front with four white windows and a blue door. But at the back, instead of a garden, there was a pretty verandah where trees like round, green lollipops stood in wooden tubs.

Gravity's Parlour was in the largest upstairs room – where she liked to sit in the window and watch all that was going on.

'Where can those two scamps of mine have got to?' she wondered.

Outside the snow clouds had rolled back and a sickle moon hung over the skylight, filling the Attic

with a powdery silver light. She heard the wind sighing far away in the Wild Wood and the rafters creaking under the weight of snow on the roof. At last her sharp ears picked up the sound of Cassity's voice.

'Grandad says you can't *kill* a Ghost, Uppy,' Cassity was saying. 'So after his last Great Battle with Malignity, he banished him. What does banished mean?'

Uppity did not know but was not going to say so.

'You must have got it wrong, Cass,' he scoffed. 'I expect Grandad said *vanished*. Anyway – I keep telling you – there's no such thing as Ghosts!'

Gravity sighed and left the window to go and meet them. When she saw them creeping wearily up the verandah steps like two black shadows in the moonlight, she thought they looked like Ghosts themselves. But she was not angry. She was too glad to see them safely home.

After Cassity had been cleaned and fed and tucked up in the nest that Gravity had made from tufts of Mrs Jones's old fur coat, Uppity told his mother about their adventures.

'I didn't mean to leave Cass for more than five shakes of my tail, Mam,' he said. 'But Uncle Serenity kept me . . .'

'Don't make excuses, Pet,' said Gravity, licking her paws which were still black from washing Cassity. 'I've warned you often enough to keep away from Serenity! He and your Pa are two of a kind! They're irresponsible!'

Many moons ago Uppity's father, Levity, had abandoned his family in the Doll's House and set up a new one in the Airing Cupboard on the landing. He was easily bored and could never take anything seriously. Sometimes Gravity worried that Uppity would turn out to be like him.

'You'd do better to follow your Uncle Dignity's example,' she said.

'Oh boring, boring!' said Uppity, twirling his tail.

He did not much like Uncle Dignity who never smiled and who seemed to have altogether forgotten what it was like to be young. What's more, he felt his mother should be more impressed with him for the way he had rescued Cassity.

'*And* I proved that there really is a secret passage from the house to the Outhouse!' he said.

'That's as maybe, Pet,' she murmured. 'But think

of what *might* have happened. You could both have been lost for ever in the chimney! And what about this Horse in the Outhouse? You were lucky it didn't trample you to death with its great clod-hopping hooves . . .'

'Oh Mam!' protested Uppity. 'It isn't a *real* Horse. It's only a block of old wood. I expect Mr J is going to chop it up for the fire!'

But even as he spoke he remembered the uneasy feeling that Trojan had given him and, in spite of himself, he shivered.

CHAPTER SIX

'Uppy, Uppy, come and look!'

Uppity yawned and uncurled himself. Hopalong Cassity was bouncing on him, bright eyed as the dawn. But it was still as dark as midnight in the Doll's House.

'All the clouds have fallen out of the sky, Uppy,' she cried. 'And they've landed on the garden! Come and see!'

Grumpily, Uppity followed her down the Doll's House stairs. A thick layer of snow lay on the skylight, blotting out the morning. Cassity led him among the dim shapes of the lumber to where spokes of daylight were poking into the Attic through the gaps under the eaves.

'See!' she said.

Uppity peered out and hardly recognized the World. Beyond the buried garden the River glided like a slow, black snake through Meadows that were as smooth and white and shining as the icing on Mrs Jones's cake. Only the dark trees in the Wild Wood showed where the earth ended and the sky began.

'It's magic, Uppy!' said Cassity.

Then she wriggled under the slates and into the

gutter, from where she could look straight down into the Yard.

'Uppy! Uppy!' she squealed. 'Trojan's come out of the Outhouse!'

Uppity crawled out beside her and looked down. Sure enough, the Horse was now standing in the middle of the Yard. Two furrows from the Outhouse door showed where his frame had been dragged through the snow. Cassity gazed at him entranced.

'He was *miserable* in there, he was,' she murmured. 'It was so dark and coaly . . .'

'Snarls!' said Uppity, who was not sure he liked being perched like a Sparrow on the gutter. 'Don't be so fanciful, Cass! He isn't *alive*!'

A flurry of snow swept across the Yard and the wind lifted the Horse's tattered mane so that it drifted out in a black cloud among the flying white flakes. His eyes were as blank as pebbles. And as the North Wind swayed him into a slow canter his lips seemed to curl back from his teeth in a snarl.

In daylight Uppity liked the Horse less than ever.

'Come back inside, Cass,' he said. 'If you stay out here the wind will blow you away. Or you'll freeze into a statue of yourself!'

Cassity argued that she wanted to stay and watch but Uppity insisted.

'Come down to the kitchen with me,' he said. 'If you hide among the plant pots on the window-ledge, you can watch him from there. At least you'll be warm. And *I* can have a good forage . . .'

Mr Jones carried a bucket of hot water from the kitchen into the Yard and began to scrub the coal dust from Trojan's head and back. Steam rose around them both like smoke and the snow in the Yard turned to a grey slush.

Later, while Mr and Mrs Jones ate their dinner, the Dog came out and yapped at the Horse. And later still, after his midday snooze, Mr Jones fetched a tin of paint and a brush. As he stroked the paint over Trojan's coat the colour came back until it shone dull silver, like the pewter plates on the kitchen dresser. He mended a tear in the saddle and poured oil on to the rusty iron rockers. Finally he brushed the Horse's mane and combed the tangles out of his tail.

At last, as the Yard filled with shadows and the slush hardened to a crinkly crust on the stones, Mr Jones wiped a drip from his nose with his scarf and went back indoors.

'Bless my soul,' said Mrs Jones, squinting through the window. 'You've made the old nag look as good as new!'

'Wish *I* was as good as new, Mrs J,' said Mr Jones, slumping into his chair by the stove. 'I'm worn out. And I don't believe it's ever *been* so cold!'

'Icebergs ahead,' screeched the Parrot. 'Remember the *Titanic*!'

'Ridiculous Bird!' said Mrs Jones. And she flung the tablecloth over the Parrot's cage. Then, giving

Mr Jones a cup of tea, she went to switch on the light and draw the curtains against the night.

Hopalong Cassity, who had fallen asleep among the pots of geraniums, woke up. A draught, needling through a crack in the window, jabbed unkindly at her. She sat up and looked once more at Trojan rocking through the dusk. His head bowed and bowed again as though a heavy weight pressed down on it.

'Poor thing,' she whispered. 'There's something wrong, there is. But *I'll* help you . . .'

Then slipping under the curtain she scuttled down the wall and set off across the floor to find Uppity.

CHAPTER SEVEN

The next morning Uppity went down to see Great-Great-Grandfather.

'Hi, Grandad!' he cried as he scampered into Serendipity's Parlour. 'D'you know anything about this Horse in the Yard?'

But Serendipity lay wheezing and sneezing on his red velvet couch and he waved him away with his paw.

'By dear Child,' he groaned. 'Don't cobe dear be! I'be caught ad awful COLD. Go and tell Dignity he must take ober for a while as Head of the Tribe.'

When Uppity delivered the message Uncle Dignity shook his head.

'Hm. Ha. Indeed!' he said. 'There seems to be some terrible blight on this house today! Why only this morning, I myself came near to Disaster! I was attempting to scratch a crispy brown crust out of the toaster when one of my claws became trapped in the works and I could not move. As I struggled to free myself the Dog began to bark and Mrs Jones came hurrying down the stairs to see what was going on. Then . . .'

'I can't stop, Uncle,' said Uppity, who knew that

Uncle Dignity could take the rest of the day to tell his story. 'Mam needs me back in the Attic!' And he scurried away as fast as he could go.

When he returned to the Doll's House his mother was looking worried.

'Have you seen Hopalong anywhere, Pet?' asked Gravity. 'She's gone missing again. I do declare I don't know what's got into her! I *knew* that Horse was Bad News! Ever since he appeared in the Outhouse, there's been trouble . . .'

'Snarls!' grumbled Uppity. 'This is getting so *boring*!'

His sister was not in the Attic so he went down to the Smallest Bedroom to see if she was with Alacrity. But neither of them was there. Then he dawdled along the landing to the Airing Cupboard where Cassity sometimes liked to rough and tumble with their half-brothers and sisters.

'Sorry, Son,' yawned his father, who was basking in the warmth of the hot water tank. 'She hasn't hopped along here for days.'

And snuffling at his own joke, Levity burrowed into a pile of sheets and disappeared.

As he pattered along the trackways in the walls which were usually thronging with Mice, Uppity met no one. There was nobody in the kitchen either. Not the Joneses. Not the Dog. Not even Uncle Serenity who hardly ever left it in case he missed a specially delicious tit bit.

Uppity mooched about wondering where to look next. He found a squishy bit of date under the table and stopped to nibble it. Then he climbed up to the window-ledge. The window was covered in a pattern of ferns and leaves as if, in the night, the Wild Wood had crept up through the Water Meadows and the garden and left its snowy prints upon the panes. But there was no sign of Cassity among the geranium pots.

Putting one eye to the clear, round centre of a frost flower, Uppity looked out. It had snowed again. And except for a path which Mr Jones had dug to the Outhouse, the snow lay everywhere deep and crisp and even. A solitary Robin pecked at the crumbs that Mrs Jones had scattered for the Sparrows, and through the branches of the apple tree a white-faced sun glared down at it.

There was nothing else at all in the Yard. Even Trojan was not there. Like everyone else, the Horse had disappeared.

CHAPTER EIGHT

Feeling cross and puzzled and lonely, Uppity made his way back to the track in the wall. As soon as he slipped through the gap in the skirting board, he could hear a soft humming noise that seemed to be coming from somewhere across the hall. From Mr and Mrs Jones's Parlour.

He headed in that direction and the noise grew steadily louder. By the time he reached the Mouse-hole under the Big Clock, he knew what it was. It was the sound made by a great crowd of Mice as they squeaked and shuffled and scampered about together.

Cautiously Uppity nosed out into the room. Although it was the middle of the day the Jones's Parlour was dim and dusky. He could hear Mice skittering about the floor and scuttling over the furniture but he could hardly see them because their grey bodies blended into the twilight.

Hanging heavy in the air was a strange, strong scent that Uppity had never smelled before. Yet he felt as if, somehow, he had always known it. There was tree bark in it and leaf mould, damp earth and pine needles. And a whiff of Owl. Fierce and raw and dangerous, it was the smell of the Wild Wood. He was just sniffing about trying to find the source of it when Uncle Serenity slouched past.

'Hey, Man,' drawled Serenity, 'what's with the Joneses today? See what they've brought into their Parlour! They're off their rockers, Man! Loopy as a bit of ravelled string . . .!'

And muttering to himself he loped away to be lost in the crowd.

Uppity moved further into the room. His paws crackled over sheets of brightly coloured paper. His claws snagged on coils of whiskery, silver string. Then he bumped into a golden ball that rolled lightly away from him across the carpet. And chasing after it he came upon the TREE.

With its top almost touching the ceiling the Tree stood in the window, blocking out most of the daylight. It was not bare and brown and wintery like the apple tree in the Yard. Its spiky branches were green as summertime and the powerful scent which flowed from them made Uppity feel giddy.

'Snarls!' he whispered.

Suddenly Homity appeared beside him.

'Oh dear!' moaned Homity. 'S-something must . . .

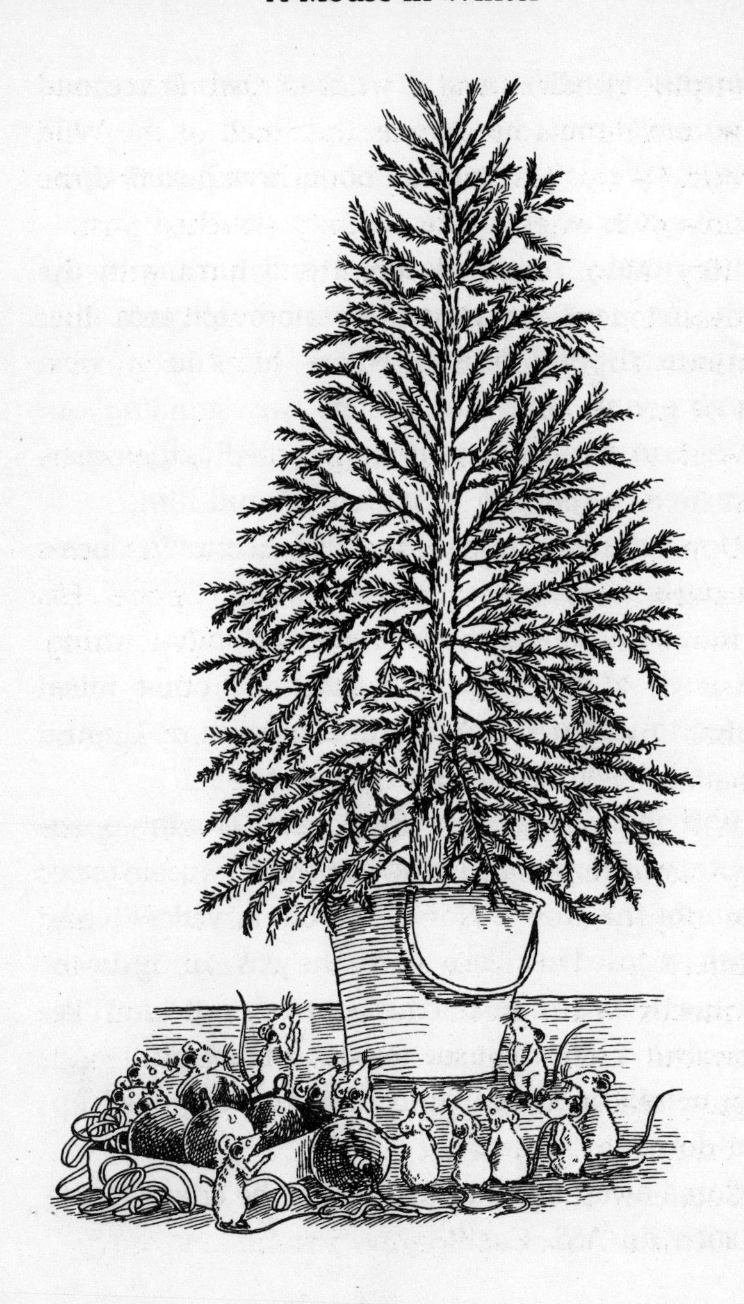

S-something *really* must . . . I mean *clearly* s-something *really* must be d-done . . .'

'What *are* you wittering about, Hom?' said Uppity. 'It's only a Tree after all!'

But Homity shook his head and turning away from the Tree he raised his nose towards the fireplace. Uppity looked where his cousin was pointing and saw that Trojan was standing on the hearth rug. And chattering excitedly, the other Mice were beginning to gather around him.

'Now what's happening?' cried Curiosity, dashing past.

Homity did not reply but nudged Uppity towards the back of the crowd. At once the other Mice parted to let them through and as soon as Uppity reached the front he could see why.

High above them, crouching inside Trojan's open mouth, was Hopalong Cassity. She did not seem to be aware of the crowd. Nor of the blunt, yellow teeth which enclosed her like a fence. She was staring down into the Horse's throat and her ears were twitching like they always did when she was listening hard.

In a mix-up of fear and fury, Uppity jigged up and down.

'Come away from there at once!' he cried. 'Don't be such an ASS, Cass!'

The other Mice uttered a gasp that was half laugh, half groan but Cassity did not stir.

'I've been looking for you all morning!' raged Uppity. 'What d'you think you're doing up there!'

'She's under a s-spell,' shuddered Homity, twisting his whiskers into a corkscrew. 'S-something evil has her in its power . . .'

Uppity snorted but Homity was shaking from head to tail and his eyes glistened as if with tears. Like Great-Great-Grandfather he was especially fond of Cassity. She reminded him of his sister Dimity who had gone out into the World to seek her fortune and had never returned . . .

'I'll fetch Uncle Dignity,' threatened Uppity. '*He'll* not stand for your nonsense!'

Dreamily Cassity raised her withered paw to her mouth.

'Sshh,' she murmured.

The Mice fell silent and the only sound was the husky tick of the Big Clock. Then, from deep inside Trojan, they all heard a snuffle and a sigh. Followed by a strange flapping sound and a long, wailing cry.

'Whatever is it?' cried Curiosity.

'I think it's the Ghost,' whispered Homity, shuddering again. 'I think MALIGNITY's come back!'

And he buried his face in his paws.

CHAPTER NINE

After that, rumours about Trojan spread like a sickness through the Mousehold. The oldest Mice took to their beds. And the youngest woke crying from nightmares about Ghosts who came galloping out of the walls, or swooped into their Parlours hooting like Owls.

Every Mouse had a tale of disaster to tell and when Great-Great-Grandfather's cold went from bad to worse every Mouse blamed it on the Horse.

Up in the Attic frost grew like mould on the undersides of the slates, and icicles, hanging from the roof, made a glassy barrier across the gaps under the eaves. The Sparrows, who usually flew freely in and out, bringing gossip and good cheer from Outside, could not get in. They sat in a dejected row along the gutter, fluffing out their feathers and cheeping miserably.

The up-and-coming young Mice huddled around the chimney breast, puffing out wisps of white steam as they talked.

'Well I'm not scared,' declared Uppity, strutting up and down. 'After all, even when Cass climbed right into Trojan's mouth nothing happened to her, did it?'

Above them, the Jackdaw who always roosted on the chimney pot, croaked loudly as the smoke got into his eyes.

'D-did you hear that?' stammered Homity. 'He said Beware! . . . B-BEWARE . . . !'

'Hickory, dickory,' said Alacrity. 'Don't take any notice of *him*! He's worse than the Parrot. He's always predicting disaster!'

'What's predicting mean?' asked Curiosity.

Alacrity, who was good at words, started to explain.

'Oh boring, boring!' said Uppity.

And he scampered off to see if Great-Great-Grandfather Serendipity was any better.

'I hear,' said Serendipity, peering at Uppity through bleary eyes, 'that everywod thigs this Horse in the Jodes's Parlour is haunted . . .'

'Huh!' said Uppity. 'They're all just frightening *themselves*! If Ghosts *did* exist they couldn't hurt us. They're only empty air!'

Serendipity coughed and sniffed and shook his head which was hot and heavy and full of ache.

'By dear Child,' he said. 'Who knows? I only

remember that whed Maligdity was here nothig ever went right in the Jodes's house. Wod DISASTER was followed by adother and there was no peace . . .'

He coughed again. The cold was making him feel his age and his aching head made thinking difficult. It was many moons since he had rid the house of Malignity and it had been a long and fearful battle. If there *was* something wicked inside the Horse, who could fight such a battle now? He believed Uppity was brave and resourceful, a future leader of the Tribe perhaps, but he was still very young and had never been tested.

He was still pondering about these things when there was a rapid pitter-patter of feet on the track outside and Alacrity skidded into his Parlour.

'Grandad!' she cried. 'Oh Grandad! Something TERRIBLE has happened!'

Then, seeing Uppity, she beckoned him with a flick of her tail.

'Quick! Quick!' she urged him. 'Come at once to the Jones's Parlour! The Horse has *swallowed* Cassity!'

CHAPTER TEN

In Mr and Mrs Jones's Parlour, the Tree from the Wild Wood was ablaze with light. Golden baubles swung in the draught from the window and loops of silver thread hung among its branches.

'Uncle Serenity told us the Tree was dressed up in jewels like a Queen,' explained Alacrity. 'So Curiosity and Homity and me came down to see . . . And when we got here we saw Cassity sitting in Trojan's mouth again!'

'One tick of the clock she was there,' said Curiosity, 'and the next she'd gone. Vanished!'

'Oh dear, oh deary!' cried Homity.

Uppity's heart was knocking hard against his ribs. Clearly his three cousins were expecting him to do something. But he did not know *what* to do. Instead of ideas all he had inside his head were pictures of his sister. Her small wistful face, her sandy coat, her funny lopsided walk. Often when she was pestering him he told her to get lost. But now that she *was* lost he realised how much he loved her.

'I'll climb up,' he croaked, 'and look inside the Horse's mouth.'

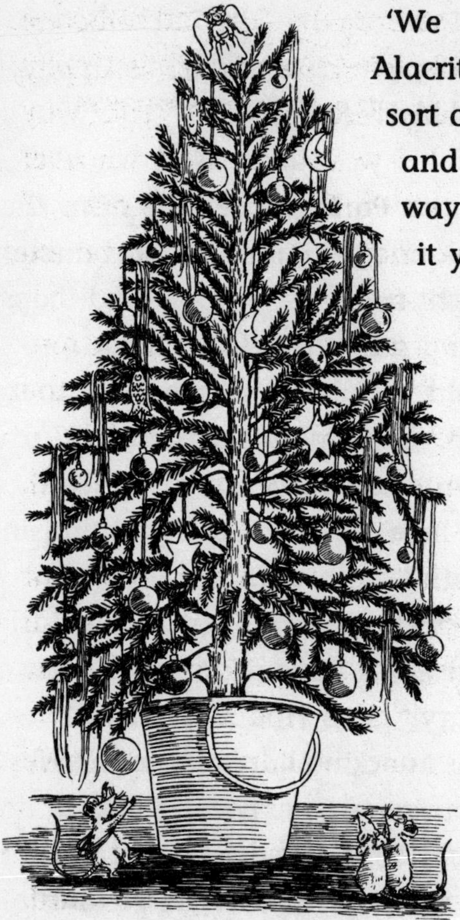

'We already did,' said Alacrity. 'But there's a sort of flap in his throat and it only opens one way. If you go through it you'll be trapped!'

'And it looks b-black er than the Cellar down there,' shuddered Homity. 'B-blacker even than the Foundations . . .'

Uppity twirled his tail impatiently. He felt that if he did not go at once he would never go. His courage would run out altogether. He glanced up at the Horse and in the glow from the Tree Trojan's dark eye seemed to glitter back at him with a mocking light.

Suddenly Alacrity, who was gazing at the Tree, gave a cry.

'I've just thought of something,' she said. 'What if

we pulled a silver thread from the Tree and someone sat in Trojan's mouth holding one end while Uppity went down into his belly with the other? That way he'd be sure to find his way back! And whoever holds the string can open the flap to let him out . . .'

'But who?' asked Curiosity. 'Who is brave enough to sit in Trojan's mouth?'

There was a long silence. Then to Uppity's astonishment, Homity said, 'I will. If . . . if *Uppity's* on the other end of the thread, *I* won't be sc-scared . . .'

He trailed to a stop and Uppity hung his head. 'Thanks, Hom,' he mumbled.

He felt ashamed. His cousins teased him for boasting about how brave he was but now it was Homity, the most fearful of them all, who was trusting him to be *truly* brave.

'Come on then,' said Alacrity. 'Hurry! We mustn't waste time!'

She whisked over to the Tree and seizing the end of a silver string in her mouth she tugged it hard. Uppity went to help and between them they dragged it free. They coiled the tinsel round Uppity's middle and then, while Curiosity and Alacrity watched from the hearthrug, Uppity and Homity climbed up towards the Horse's head.

In the angle between Trojan's foreleg and his

chest they paused to rest. And from deep inside the Horse they heard a cry. It was very faint and far away but they both knew at once who it was.

'Cass!' said Uppity.

'Oh dear!' murmured Homity.

Shakily they started off again, clambering up through the strands of the Horse's mane. When they reached his mouth, Homity took one end of the silver thread and tucked it beneath him as he curled up in the hollow behind Trojan's teeth. Then he shut his eyes tight for fear of what he might see.

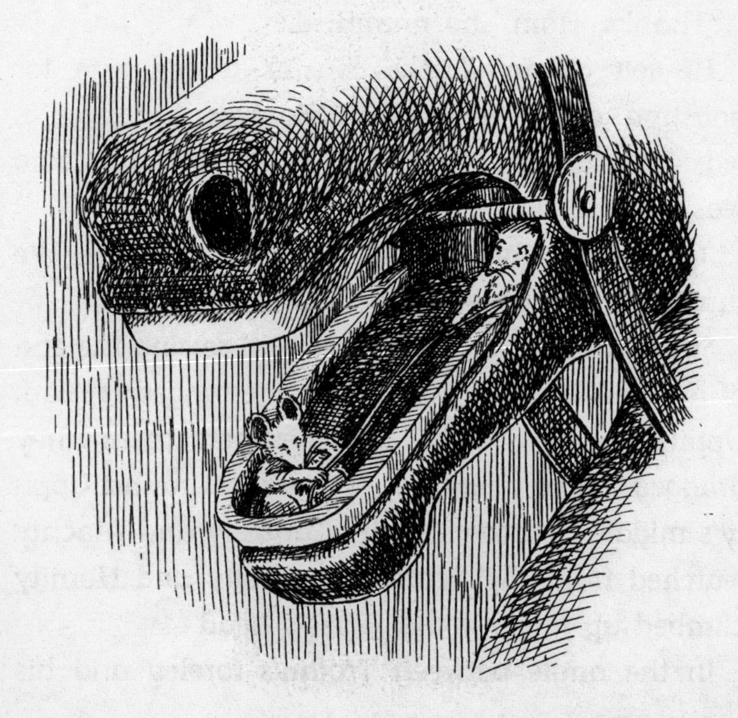

'Don't fall asleep, Hom!' said Uppity.

Except for a twitch on the thread there was no response.

Trying to make himself feel as brave as Great-Great-Grandfather Serendipity, Uppity puffed out his chest and then went down to the flap. It opened easily. He nosed through it and it closed behind him with a sigh. A cold, musty smell breathed up at him from the depths. Half running, half sliding he began to descend the Horse's gullet.

CHAPTER ELEVEN

The gullet soon came to an end and Uppity dropped into a hollow space. Here, the slight, silvery radiance shed by the tinsel only seemed to make the darkness worse. And as he wandered out into it, with the thread unwinding behind him, he could hear the echoes of his own movement, whispering all round him.

'Cass!' he called. 'Are you there, Cass?'

Somewhere – he could not tell where – he thought he heard a scuffling sound. But nothing except the echo answered his call. He went on. The air inside Trojan was stale and stuffy. And icy cold. Hadn't Grandad said something about Malignity breathing out a cold that froze Mice to the bone?

To comfort himself he took the thread between his teeth and tweaked it hard. Immediately he felt Homity's answering tug. The whiskery string shivered between them, shaking out little darts of light. As the darts disappeared into the blackness, the shadows that lurked there seemed to shuffle nearer . . .

'Scram!' he growled, boxing at the shadows. 'Get away!'

He was sure his paws had not touched anything but the air was suddenly filled with twittering noises. Uppity twirled round and round trying to see what it was that flittered about him, weaving unseen patterns in the dark.

'Who's there?' he cried. 'Wh-who are you?'

'Oooo . . . aaah . . . oooo,' came the echo.

As he turned again the last of the tinsel unwound from his middle and he had to jump on it to stop it from slipping away. More sparks of light shook out of it. Only a whisker's length away the sparks glinted back at him out of two round, frightened eyes. And glimmered on a pale, sand-coloured coat . . .

'Cass!' he cried.

'Uppy?' His sister's voice quavered uncertainly. 'Oh Uppy!' she said. 'How you scared me! Twirling about – all shimmery and shiny like that! I thought you were the Ghost!'

'*Me* the Ghost!' exclaimed Uppity. He looked up to where the invisible Thing still swooped and swerved over their heads. 'What about *that*?' he said.

To his surprise, Cassity giggled.

'That's only poor Pippin,' she said.

When Uppity did not reply, she crept closer to him and nuzzled his ear gently.

'Pippin's a Bat,' she whispered. 'From the Wild Wood!'

'Huh!' said Uppity. 'I knew it wasn't Malignity. Of course I did! . . . But how did a Bat from the Wild Wood get into Trojan's belly?'

'Well,' began Cassity, 'he was all snuggled down for the Winter in a Hollow Tree when a Man came and chopped the tree down . . .'

'Snarls!' said Uppity.

'And the next thing he knew,' Cassity went on, 'he was in Mr Jones's woodpile. He was crawling about, all snoozy and woozy still, when he tumbled down Trojan's throat . . .'

'And was trapped . . .'

'Yes,' agreed Cassity. 'He kept calling for help but nobody would listen.'

'Except you,' said Uppity.

For the second time that night he felt ashamed.

'Just the same,' he said, 'you shouldn't have come down here on your own!'

His sister giggled again.

'I didn't really mean to, Uppy,' she said. 'But *I* tumbled too, I did!'

CHAPTER TWELVE

In the Jones's Parlour, Alacrity and Curiosity were playing I Spy to keep themselves awake. Outside, the snow fluttered against the window and in the chimney the North Wind whiffled softly. They heard Mr and Mrs Jones talking in the kitchen and soon afterwards the Big Clock over the Mouse-hole began the strokes of twelve.

'Hickory, dickory!' said Alacrity. 'Uppity's been gone a long time!'

'Whatever d'you suppose has happened?' yawned Curiosity, who was longing for sleep.

Above them in Trojan's mouth, Homity jumped as an urgent tapping and scratching started up behind the flap.

'Is that you, Uppity?' he whispered.

But if there was an answer he could not hear it for the striking of the clock.

'M-mustn't think about M-Malignity,' Homity said to himself. 'Think of Uppity . . . think of *Hopalong* . . .'

So reciting her name like a charm he nudged at the flap with his nose. It did not budge. Taking a deep breath he tried once more. This time he pushed so hard that it flew open and he shot headfirst into Uppity who was right behind it.

Uppity pushed him back and scrambled through. Then Homity saw Cassity's bright eyes peeping through the flap and he rushed forward again to welcome her. In the muddle of them all milling about in the back of Trojan's throat, he did not notice the shadowy, Mouse-like creature which crawled through after her until it tried to brush between them.

'Help!' he squealed. 'Help! Malignity's escaped! Help!'

'Don't be such a nincompoop, Hom!' exclaimed

Uppity, forgetting his resolution to be kind to his cousin.

The Bat gave a little grunt and went steadily on. Watching from below, Alacrity and Curiosity saw him hang from the Horse's lower lip for a moment and then drop. His dark, velvety wings unfolded and he flitted silently towards the Tree.

Then, as Uppity, Cassity and Homity slid one after the other down Trojan's frame, the latch on the Parlour door rattled and lifted. Scattering in all directions, the five Mice fled under the sofa and behind the chairs. While the Bat went flickering wildly about the room, Mr and Mrs Jones came in with their arms full of parcels.

'Dang and drat the Bat!' huffed Mr Jones, flapping at Pippin with his handkerchief.

'Stop cussing, Mr J,' said Mrs Jones. 'At least we've got him as far as the kitchen. Now keep calm, do!'

'Calm?' shrieked the Parrot, as the Bat swooped round and round her. '*What* calm?'

She bobbed furiously up and down until her cage was pitching and tossing like a boat on a rough sea.

'It's making me seasick,' she croaked. 'Sick as a Parrot!'

'Quiet!' barked the Dog. 'Quiet! . . . Quiet!'

Mr Jones sank into his rocking chair and mopped his face. Outside the North Wind roared away over the rooftops and a few last snowflakes drifted in through the wide open door. The Bat flew in another circle.

'Douse the lights!' squawked the Parrot. 'Douse the lights!'

Mr Jones, too tired to argue, reached up and pressed the switch. The moon sailed from between the clouds and smiled down into the Yard. And with a little, trilling song, the Bat dipped under the door frame and soared towards it.

CHAPTER THIRTEEN

The next day the sun blazed from a clear, blue sky and the whole World sparkled and shone. Icicles hanging from the eaves melted away and the Sparrows flew into the Attic squabbling and gossiping and twittering with laughter. In his Parlour behind the stove, Great-Great-Grandfather Serendipity felt like a new Mouse because his cold had gone.

'Moons and moons in me yet,' he muttered as he licked the white fur on his belly till it darkened to a youthful grey.

Then he sent for Uppity.

'My dear Child,' he said. 'You have shown great courage and daring in rescuing your sister. What's more, you have freed the Horse – and the House – from an EVIL INFLUENCE . . .'

'Actually, Grandad,' said Uppity, 'it wasn't exactly . . . I mean, it had nothing to do with *Malignity*. Trojan just had a Bat in his belly . . .'

'Bats in the belfry?' said Serendipity, who was deafer than usual from the after effects of his cold. 'What have they got to do with it?'

But without waiting for Uppity to answer he rushed on again.

'The sun's shining and all's well with the World,' he said. 'We must CELEBRATE! I think we should have a PARTY!'

A little later the whole Mousehold buzzed with excitement as Uppity scurried from the Attic to the Cellar with Serendipity's message.

'Man!' said Uncle Serenity, sniffing the delicious herby and spicy smells that were wafting around the kitchen. 'Don't I just DIG Parties!'

And with a wiggle of his bottom and a shake of his tail, he went shimmying out to forage.

By the time Uppity had told everyone about the Party, the sun was already tilting towards the West. As he nipped into the kitchen for a quick snack, he saw a small Boy with eyes as blue as the summer sky come skipping through the door.

'Merry Chris-Mouse, Gran and Grandad,' he heard the Boy shout.

'Merry Chris-Mouse, Harry!' said Mr and Mrs Jones.

'Can I go and play in the Parlour?' asked Harry.

'Not today, Pet,' said Mr and Mrs Jones, smiling and winking at each other. 'You must wait for tomorrow. There's a BIG SURPRISE in there for you . . .'

When the moon stood high over the skylight, the Mice crept out of every nook and cranny of the house. As they filed out of the Mousehole under the Big Clock in the Jones's Parlour, they too had a big surprise. A low fire was burning in the grate and in its warmth the dangerous Wild Wood smell of the Tree had faded right away. Lights twinkled like stars among its branches and brightly coloured boxes were piled around its roots.

On the table there were bowls heaped with apples and oranges and dishes full of nuts and sweet black raisins. And just inside the hearth, beside a glass of something that sparkled like water but smelled of grapes and sunshine, there were two of Mrs Jones's mince pies.

'No one is to touch those,' said Uppity importantly. 'Grandad says they're for Santa Claws . . .'

Then, while Great-Great-Grandfather slumbered by the embers of the fire, Uppity and Cassity, Alacrity, Curiosity and Homity and all the other up-and-coming young Mice played Hide and Seek and Hunt the Raisin. They jived on the table and jigged on the carpet. They swung on Trojan's tail and scampered all over his back till they rocked him into a canter. They frolicked and foraged until they were so tired and so full that they dropped asleep where they stood.

At last only Uppity was left awake.

'That was the BEST Party ever,' he yawned as he wandered across the room to find Cassity.

She was curled up on the hearth rug with her back against the Horse's frame. As he settled down beside her she raised her head.

'Trojan's happy now, he is,' she mumbled sleepily. 'And poor Pippin is free. Thank you for rescuing us, Uppy. You're so *brave*, you are . . . !'

'Snarls!' said Uppity. 'It was nothing!'

From somewhere above them he heard a faint snicker of laughter. And looking up as a last yellow flame spurted from the fire, he thought he saw Trojan's lips curl back in a smile and his dark eye droop in a friendly wink.

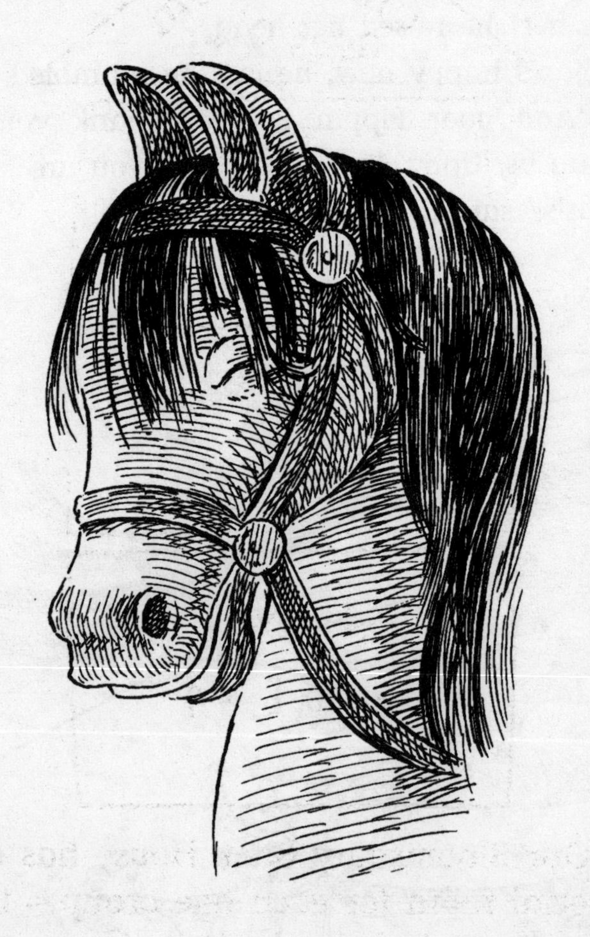

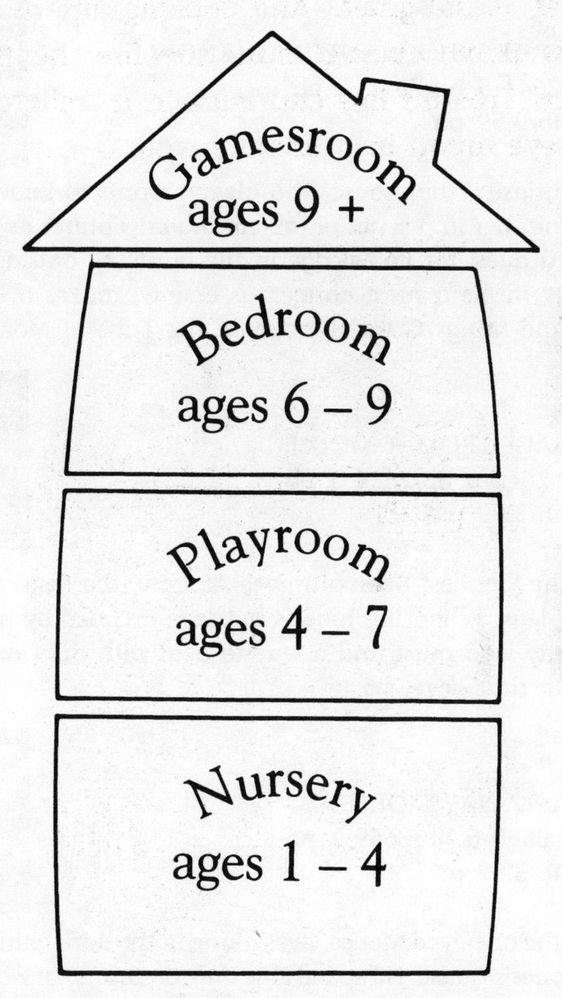

Our Bloomsbury Book House has a special room for each age group – this one is from the Bedroom.

Watch out for more MOUSE TALES by Anne Merrick:

THE MOUSE WHO WANTED TO KNOW
07475 2641 9 hb/2615 X pb
£6.99 hb/3.99 pb

Meet Curiosity, the mouse who always wants to know everything! Join her in a series of tail-curling adventures as she sets out on a quest for knowledge in the terrifying outside world. Curiosity meets a most dangerous enemy, makes a life-long friend and brings Great Honour on the Tribe of Mousity.

A MESSAGE FROM A MOUSE
0 7475 2640 0 hb/2614 1 pb
£6.99 hb/3.99 pb

Up in the Smallest Bedroom lives Alacrity, the fastest mouse on four legs. When the Jones's house is invaded by a Boy, it is Alacrity who must find a way to deal with the Dangerous Situation that develops.

THE CASTAWAY MOUSE
0 7475 2660 5 hb/2659 1 pb
£6.99 hb/3.99 pb

Oddity the one-eyed Mouse, lives alone in the dark foundations of the Jones's house. He spends his time dreaming of wonderful and mysterious Other Worlds – and his sweetheart, Dimity. Then one terrible day in November, there is a Great Flood. Join Oddity as he is carried far away from his tree-root home and has a magical adventure that changes his life forever.